Can you keep a secret? You can? GOOD.

This book will share with you the secrets of some special little animals called teezles who are so clever they could almost be called magic.

These happy little creatures live in Crabapple Wood, where they build their underground homes beneath large trees. They get their surnames from the tree under which they live.

They live in peace with all other animals, insects and birds and help them when they are injured, sick or in need.

Although teezles use nature's gifts in many wonderful ways, they always protect and preserve the countryside.

So! If you are good and kind and always care for the wonderful things that life gives to us then, maybe one day, you could become a friend of the teezles.

"GO JOYFULLY" THROUGH LIFE

THE TEEZLES and the POLLUTED POND

by Terry Barber

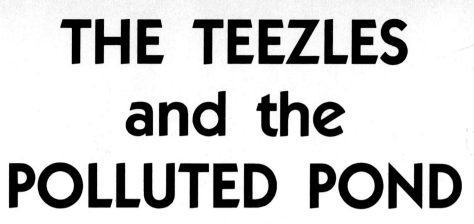

Published by Peter Haddock Limited,
Bridlington, England.

Illustrated by Wizard Art,
courtesy of Bernard Thornton Artists, London.

THE TEEZLES and the POLLUTED POND

One sunny morning, as Fern Oak and his wife, Silk, came out from their home beneath the oak tree, they saw a grey heron flying swiftly towards them. "Come quickly," gasped the bird. "Millers Pond has been poisoned and many creatures are in distress." Fern turned to his wife and told her to gather all the teezles together and go at once to the pond.

As Silk hurried off the heron called, "Jump on, Mr Oak. I will give you a ride. It will save some time." Fern hopped nimbly on to the bird's back and off they flew, following the stream that flowed from Crabapple Wood to the pond.

When they arrived, Fern immediately saw the cause of the trouble. A metal drum lay at the edge of the pond, with the words 'INSECTICIDE' and 'POISON' painted in red. The local farmer had been spraying his crops and had foolishly thrown the drum into the pond, thus spilling the remains of its deadly contents into the water.

Several dead fish and insects were floating on the surface. Water voles sat at the water's edge coughing and rubbing their eyes. Frogs, newts and fish lay in the shallow water gasping for breath. Mrs Toad sat with tears streaming down her face, while her four youngsters, with ugly white blisters on their skins, lay still on the grass, hardly breathing.

"Don't worry, help is on the way," said Fern, gently patting Mrs Toad's head. He realised that these poor creatures would all die if they were not put into pure, clean water very soon.

Before long the other teezles arrived and Fern set them all to work. Some of them had brought containers filled with fresh water and they gently lifted their sick friends into them and carried them to safety.

The female teezles tended the sick and injured. The voles and toads were carried or led upstream and bathed in clean water. Silk Oak rubbed a cool, chickweed cream on the young toads to cure their blisters, while Fern's mother, Cosy Beech, gave out herbal medicine.

Fern Oak and his wise, old father, Linden Beech, the chief teezle of Crabapple Wood, were standing by the pond when the heron and his mate joined them. Mrs Heron had a piece of string in her beak. "We have a plan to remove the drum," said the heron, "and if it works, we may also teach the farmer a lesson for causing all this trouble."

The herons flew across the pond. They skilfully threaded the string through the handle of the drum and flew off with it hanging between them.

The farmer looked up in amazement as the birds flew towards him and you can imagine his surprise when they released the drum directly above him.

He ran into his house screaming
with terror as the drum crashed to
the ground just behind him. "Serve
him right," laughed the herons.
"That will teach him to be more
careful with his poisons in the
future."

The teezles decided that the pool must be emptied to allow the poisoned water to drain away and the only way to do this was to build a dam across the stream.

Linden Beech led them to an old tree which had been partly blown down in the winter gales causing it to hang over the water. "We must dig round the base of the tree so that it will fall and block the stream," said the old teezle. "Our friends, the moles, voles and rabbits, are the best diggers in the world. Go and find them and ask them to help us."

Very soon, an army of small animals was furiously digging and, when evening came, the tree slowly fell into the stream, making a perfect dam. All the animals cheered.

Within a few days all the sick creatures were well again and the poisoned water had drained away. The pond began to fill up again; in fact the stream now had two ponds.

All the animals and birds who had helped, gathered to watch the youngsters playing together.

"It is wonderful to see everyone fit and well again, especially the children. Look, they are playing leap-frog together," said Silk Oak. Mrs Toad chuckled, "I think you mean leap-toad, don't you?" Everyone burst into laughter.

Peace and happiness had once again returned to Millers Pond.

FAMILY QUEST

All the family must sit quietly near a pond, stream or river and make a list of how many different birds, animals and insects you see.

FAMILY QUESTION

What do frogs and toads eat?

If you don't know, go to your local library and look for a book to help you find out.